W9-CGK-510

THE MARVELOUS LAND OF OZ

VOL. 7

ADAPTED FROM THE NOVEL BY L. FRANK BAUM

Writer: ERIC SHANOWER
Artist: SKOTTIE YOUNG
Colorist: JEAN-FRANCOIS BEAULIEU
Letterer: JEFF ECKLEBERRY

Assistant Editor: MICHAEL HORWITZ
Editor: NATE COSBY

Collection Editor: MARK D. BEAZLEY
Assistant Editors: ALEX STARBUCK & NELSON RIBEIRO
Editor, Special Projects: JENNIFER GRÜNWALD
Senior Editor, Special Projects: JEFF YOUNGQUIST
SVP of Print & Digital Publishing Sales: DAVID GABRIEL
Production: JERRY KALINOWSKI
Book Design: ARLENE SO

Editor in Chief: AXEL ALONSO
Chief Creative Officer: JOE QUESADA
Publisher: DAN BUCKLEY
Executive Producer: ALAN FINE

visit us at www.abdopublishing.com

Reinforced library bound edition published in 2014 by Spotlight, a division of the ABDO Group, PO Box 398166, Minneapolis, Minnesota 55439. Spotlight produces high-quality reinforced library bound editions for schools and libraries. Published by agreement with Marvel Characters, Inc.

Printed in the United States of America, North Mankato, Minnesota.
102013
012014
This book contains at least 10% recycled materials.

Library of Congress Cataloging-in-Publication Data

Shanower, Eric.
The marvelous land of Oz / adapted from the novel by L. Frank Baum ; writer: Eric Shanower ; artist: Skottie Young. -- Reinforced library bound edition.
pages cm
"Marvel."
Summary: When the Scarecrow, now the ruler of the Emerald City, is driven out by General Jinjur and her all-girl army, his friends--the Tin Woodman, a boy named Tip, and Jack Pumpkinhead--try to restore peace in this graphic novel adaptation of L. Frank Baum's classic tale.
ISBN 978-1-61479-235-2 (vol. 1) -- ISBN 978-1-61479-236-9 (vol. 2) -- ISBN 978-1-61479-237-6 (vol. 3) -- ISBN 978-1-61479-238-3 (vol. 4) -- ISBN 978-1-61479-239-0 (vol. 5) -- ISBN 978-1-61479-240-6 (vol. 6) -- ISBN 978-1-61479-241-3 (vol. 7) -- ISBN 978-1-61479-242-0 (vol. 8)
1. Graphic novels. [1. Graphic novels. 2. Fantasy.] I. Young, Skottie, illustrator. II. Baum, L. Frank (Lyman Frank), 1856-1919. Marvelous land of Oz. III. Title.
PZ7.7.S453Mar 2014
741.5'973--dc23

2013030127

Spotlight

All Spotlight books are reinforced library binding and manufactured in the United States of America.

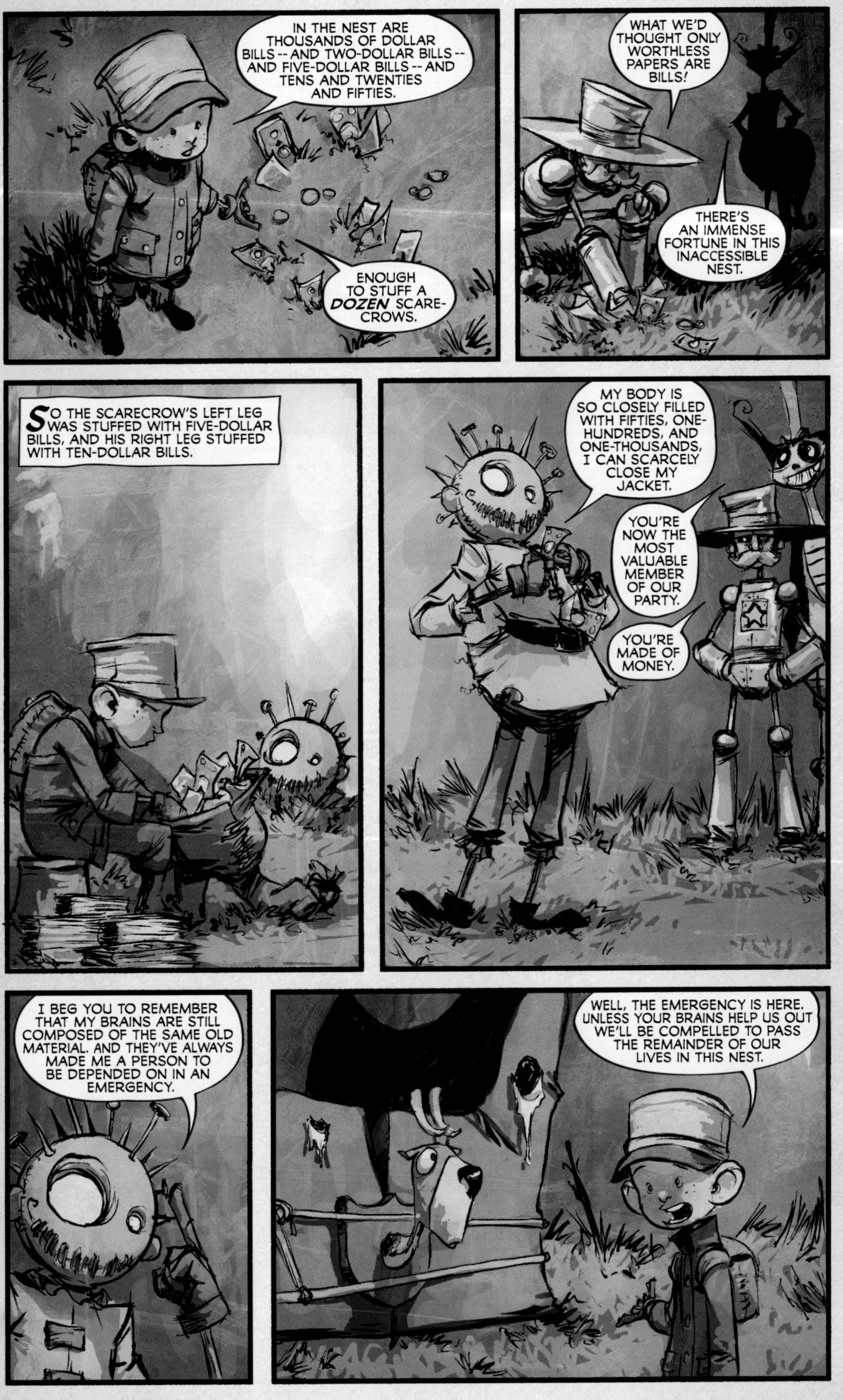
IN THE NEST ARE THOUSANDS OF DOLLAR BILLS -- AND TWO-DOLLAR BILLS -- AND FIVE-DOLLAR BILLS -- AND TENS AND TWENTIES AND FIFTIES.
ENOUGH TO STUFF A *DOZEN* SCARE-CROWS.
WHAT WE'D THOUGHT ONLY WORTHLESS PAPERS ARE BILLS!
THERE'S AN IMMENSE FORTUNE IN THIS INACCESSIBLE NEST.
SO THE SCARECROW'S LEFT LEG WAS STUFFED WITH FIVE-DOLLAR BILLS, AND HIS RIGHT LEG STUFFED WITH TEN-DOLLAR BILLS.
MY BODY IS SO CLOSELY FILLED WITH FIFTIES, ONE-HUNDREDS, AND ONE-THOUSANDS, I CAN SCARCELY CLOSE MY JACKET.
YOU'RE NOW THE MOST VALUABLE MEMBER OF OUR PARTY.
YOU'RE MADE OF MONEY.
I BEG YOU TO REMEMBER THAT MY BRAINS ARE STILL COMPOSED OF THE SAME OLD MATERIAL. AND THEY'VE ALWAYS MADE ME A PERSON TO BE DEPENDED ON IN AN EMERGENCY.
WELL, THE EMERGENCY IS HERE. UNLESS YOUR BRAINS HELP US OUT WE'LL BE COMPELLED TO PASS THE REMAINDER OF OUR LIVES IN THIS NEST.

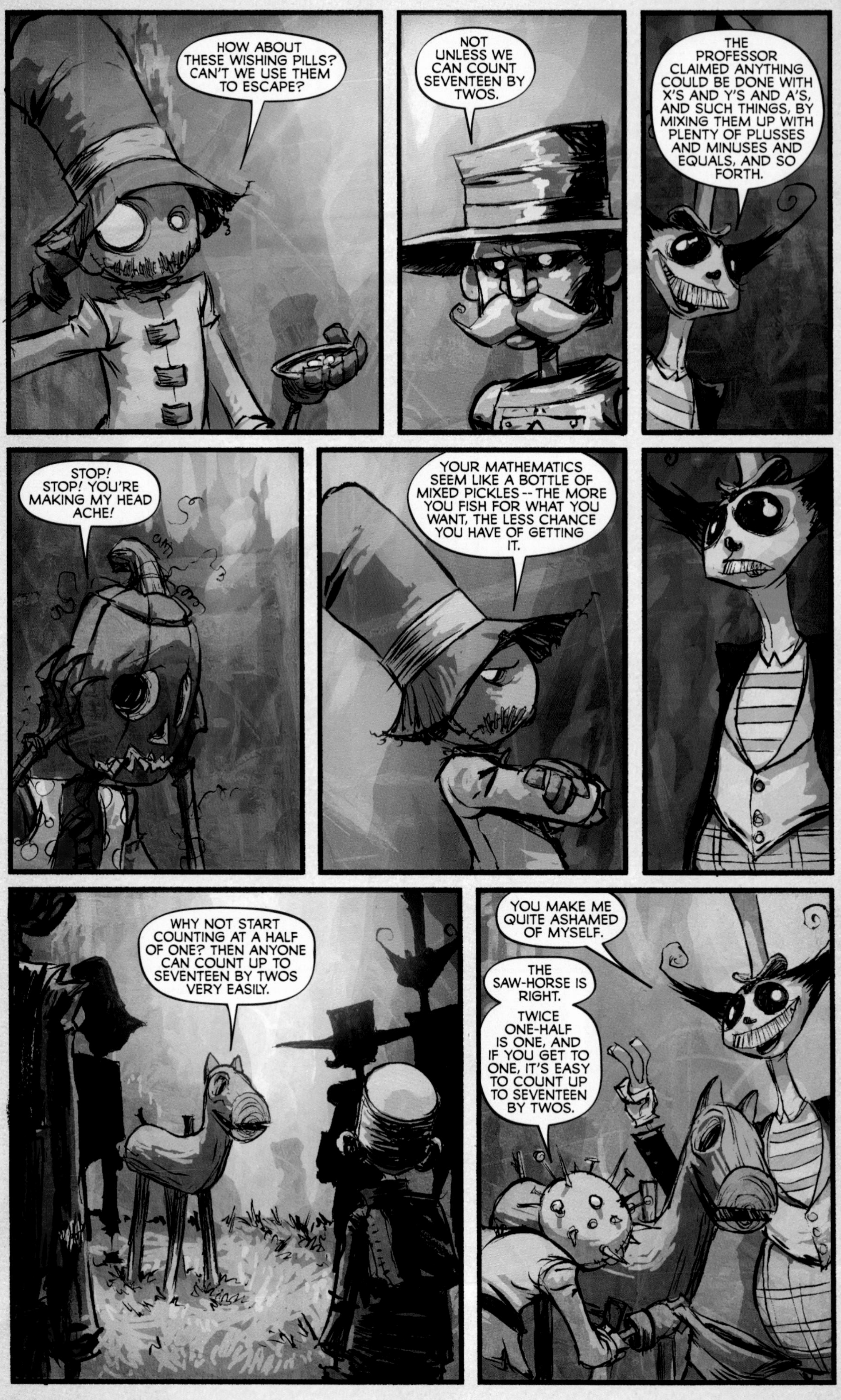
HOW ABOUT THESE WISHING PILLS? CAN'T WE USE THEM TO ESCAPE?
NOT UNLESS WE CAN COUNT SEVENTEEN BY TWOS.
THE PROFESSOR CLAIMED ANYTHING COULD BE DONE WITH X'S AND Y'S AND A'S, AND SUCH THINGS, BY MIXING THEM UP WITH PLENTY OF PLUSSES AND MINUSES AND EQUALS, AND SO FORTH.
STOP! STOP! YOU'RE MAKING MY HEAD ACHE!
YOUR MATHEMATICS SEEM LIKE A BOTTLE OF MIXED PICKLES -- THE MORE YOU FISH FOR WHAT YOU WANT, THE LESS CHANCE YOU HAVE OF GETTING IT.
WHY NOT START COUNTING AT A HALF OF ONE? THEN ANYONE CAN COUNT UP TO SEVENTEEN BY TWOS VERY EASILY.
YOU MAKE ME QUITE ASHAMED OF MYSELF.
THE SAW-HORSE IS RIGHT.
TWICE ONE-HALF IS ONE, AND IF YOU GET TO ONE, IT'S EASY TO COUNT UP TO SEVENTEEN BY TWOS.

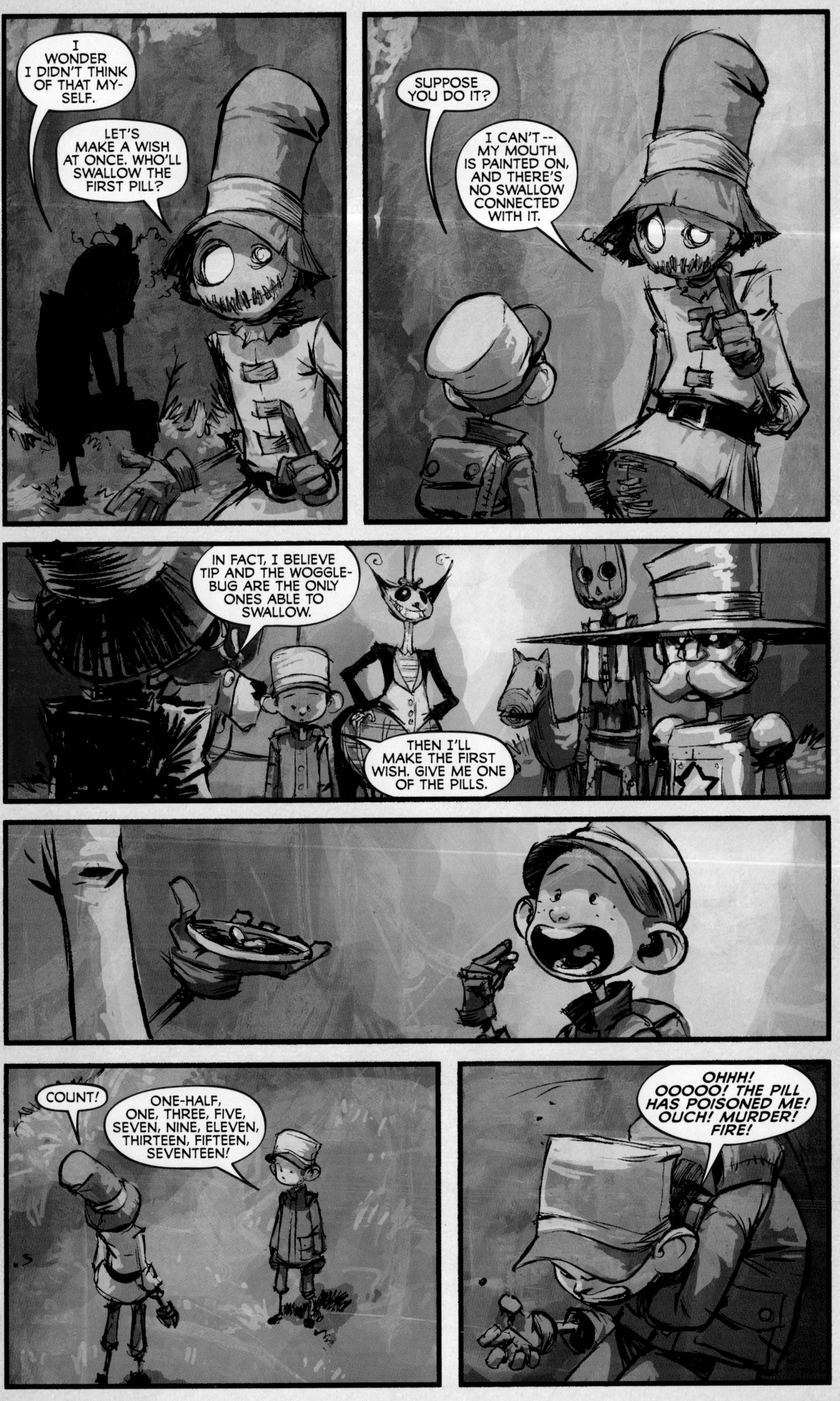
I WONDER I DIDN'T THINK OF THAT MY-SELF.
LET'S MAKE A WISH AT ONCE. WHO'LL SWALLOW THE FIRST PILL?
SUPPOSE YOU DO IT?
I CAN'T -- MY MOUTH IS PAINTED ON, AND THERE'S NO SWALLOW CONNECTED WITH IT.
IN FACT, I BELIEVE TIP AND THE WOGGLE-BUG ARE THE ONLY ONES ABLE TO SWALLOW.
THEN I'LL MAKE THE FIRST WISH. GIVE ME ONE OF THE PILLS.
COUNT!
ONE-HALF, ONE, THREE, FIVE, SEVEN, NINE, ELEVEN, THIRTEEN, FIFTEEN, SEVENTEEN!
OHHH! OOOOO! THE PILL HAS POISONED ME! OUCH! MURDER! FIRE!

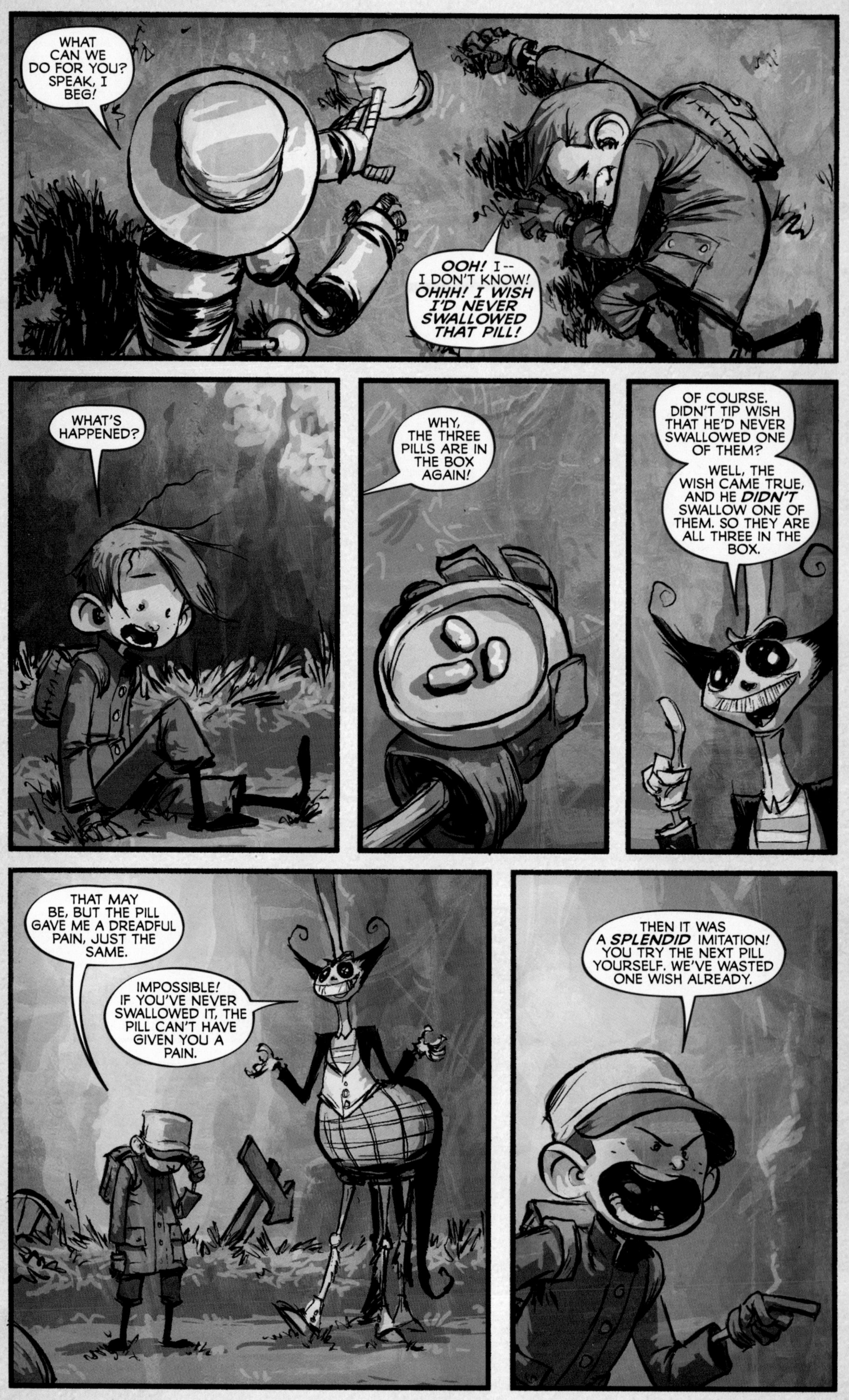

WHAT CAN WE DO FOR YOU? SPEAK, I BEG!
OOH! I -- I DON'T KNOW! OHHH! I WISH I'D NEVER SWALLOWED THAT PILL!
WHAT'S HAPPENED?
WHY, THE THREE PILLS ARE IN THE BOX AGAIN!
OF COURSE. DIDN'T TIP WISH THAT HE'D NEVER SWALLOWED ONE OF THEM?
WELL, THE WISH CAME TRUE, AND HE DIDN'T SWALLOW ONE OF THEM. SO THEY ARE ALL THREE IN THE BOX.
THAT MAY BE, BUT THE PILL GAVE ME A DREADFUL PAIN, JUST THE SAME.
IMPOSSIBLE! IF YOU'VE NEVER SWALLOWED IT, THE PILL CAN'T HAVE GIVEN YOU A PAIN.
THEN IT WAS A SPLENDID IMITATION! YOU TRY THE NEXT PILL YOURSELF. WE'VE WASTED ONE WISH ALREADY.

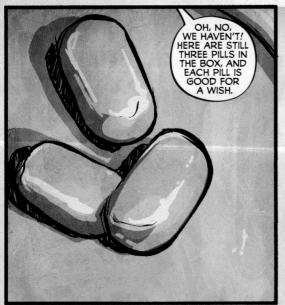

OH, NO, WE HAVEN'T! HERE ARE STILL THREE PILLS IN THE BOX, AND EACH PILL IS GOOD FOR A WISH.

NOW YOU'RE MAKING *MY* HEAD ACHE.

IT REMAINS FOR ME TO SAVE US IN MY MOST HIGHLY MAGNIFIED AND THOROUGHLY EDUCATED MANNER.

THE INSECT COUNTED SEVENTEEN BY TWOS, AND -- PERHAPS BECAUSE WOGGLE-BUGS HAVE STRONGER STOMACHS THAN BOYS -- THE SILVER PELLET CAUSED NO PAIN.

I WISH THE GUMP'S BROKEN WINGS MENDED AND AS GOOD AS NEW!

HOORAY!

WE CAN LEAVE THIS MISERABLE NEST WHENEVER WE PLEASE.

IT'S NEARLY DARK. I DON'T LIKE THESE NIGHT TRIPS, FOR ONE NEVER KNOWS WHAT WILL HAPPEN.

IT WAS DECIDED TO WAIT UNTIL DAYLIGHT. THE ADVENTURERS AMUSED THEMSELVES BY SEARCHING THE NEST FOR TREASURES.

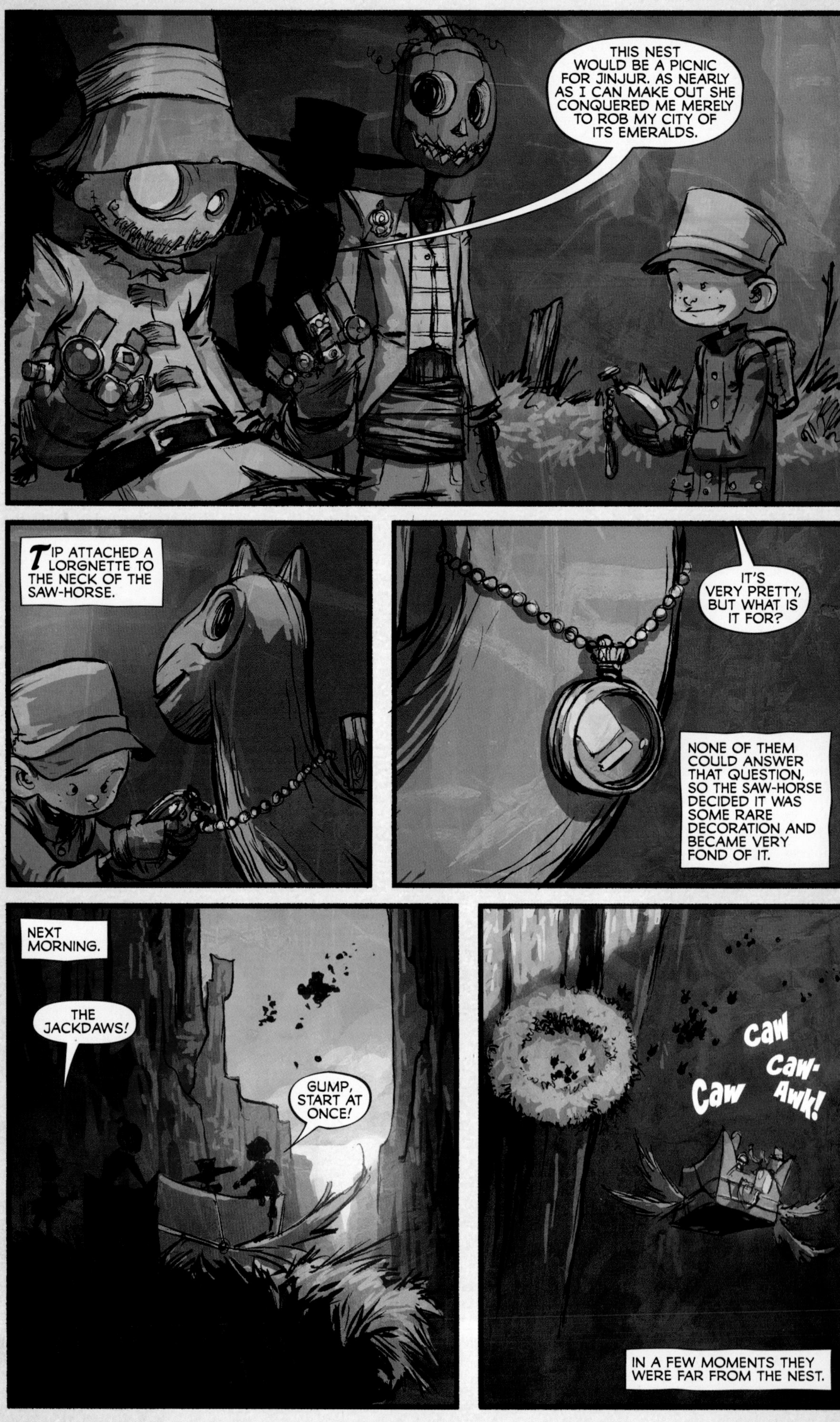
THIS NEST WOULD BE A PICNIC FOR JINJUR. AS NEARLY AS I CAN MAKE OUT SHE CONQUERED ME MERELY TO ROB MY CITY OF ITS EMERALDS.
TIP ATTACHED A LORGNETTE TO THE NECK OF THE SAW-HORSE.
IT'S VERY PRETTY, BUT WHAT IS IT FOR?
NONE OF THEM COULD ANSWER THAT QUESTION, SO THE SAW-HORSE DECIDED IT WAS SOME RARE DECORATION AND BECAME VERY FOND OF IT.
NEXT MORNING.
THE JACKDAWS!
GUMP, START AT ONCE!
Caw
Caw
Caw-Awk!
IN A FEW MOMENTS THEY WERE FAR FROM THE NEST.

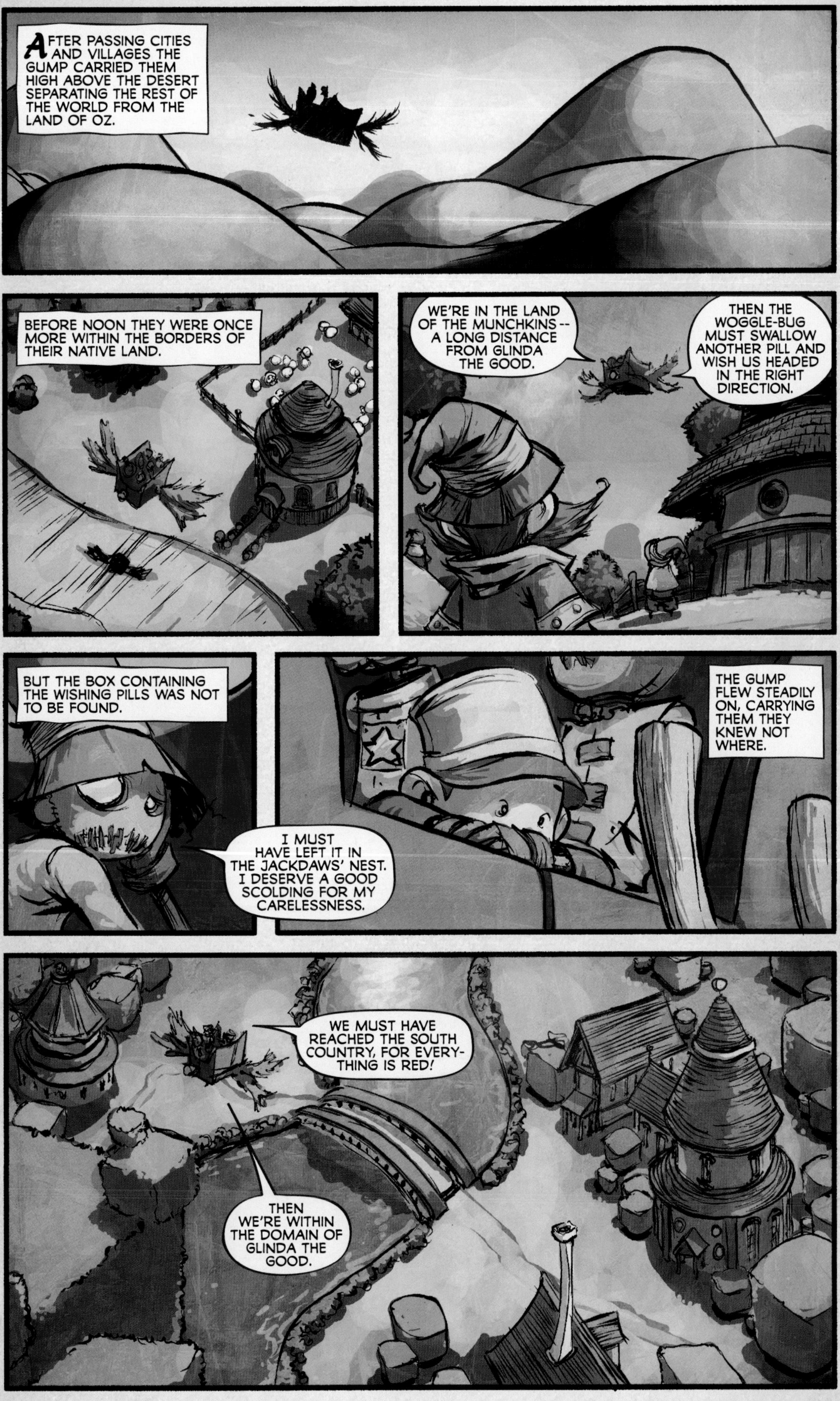
AFTER PASSING CITIES AND VILLAGES THE GUMP CARRIED THEM HIGH ABOVE THE DESERT SEPARATING THE REST OF THE WORLD FROM THE LAND OF OZ.
BEFORE NOON THEY WERE ONCE MORE WITHIN THE BORDERS OF THEIR NATIVE LAND.
WE'RE IN THE LAND OF THE MUNCHKINS -- A LONG DISTANCE FROM GLINDA THE GOOD.
THEN THE WOGGLE-BUG MUST SWALLOW ANOTHER PILL AND WISH US HEADED IN THE RIGHT DIRECTION.
BUT THE BOX CONTAINING THE WISHING PILLS WAS NOT TO BE FOUND.
I MUST HAVE LEFT IT IN THE JACKDAWS' NEST. I DESERVE A GOOD SCOLDING FOR MY CARELESSNESS.
THE GUMP FLEW STEADILY ON, CARRYING THEM THEY KNEW NOT WHERE.
WE MUST HAVE REACHED THE SOUTH COUNTRY, FOR EVERY-THING IS RED!
THEN WE'RE WITHIN THE DOMAIN OF GLINDA THE GOOD.

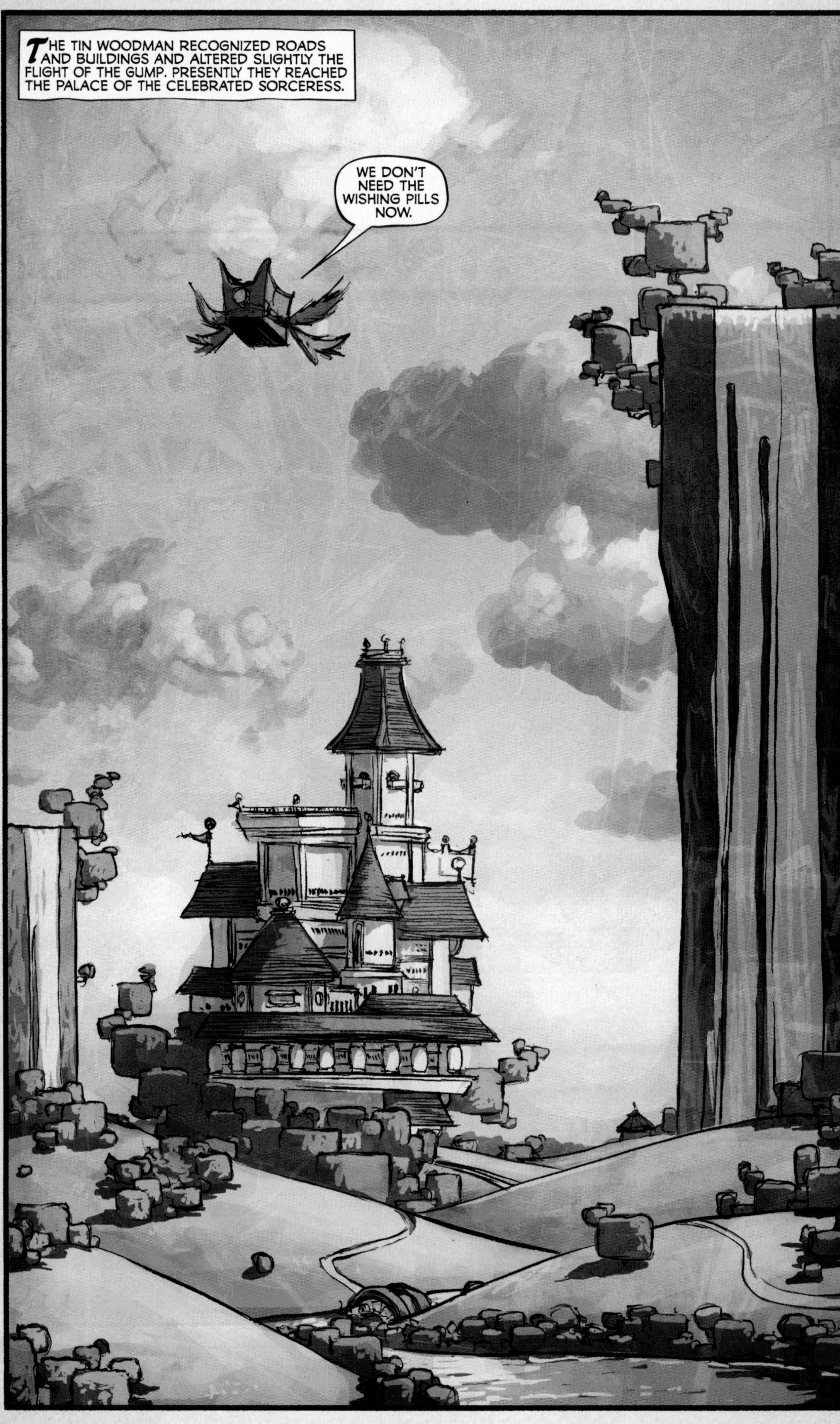
THE TIN WOODMAN RECOGNIZED ROADS AND BUILDINGS AND ALTERED SLIGHTLY THE FLIGHT OF THE GUMP. PRESENTLY THEY REACHED THE PALACE OF THE CELEBRATED SORCERESS.
WE DON'T NEED THE WISHING PILLS NOW.

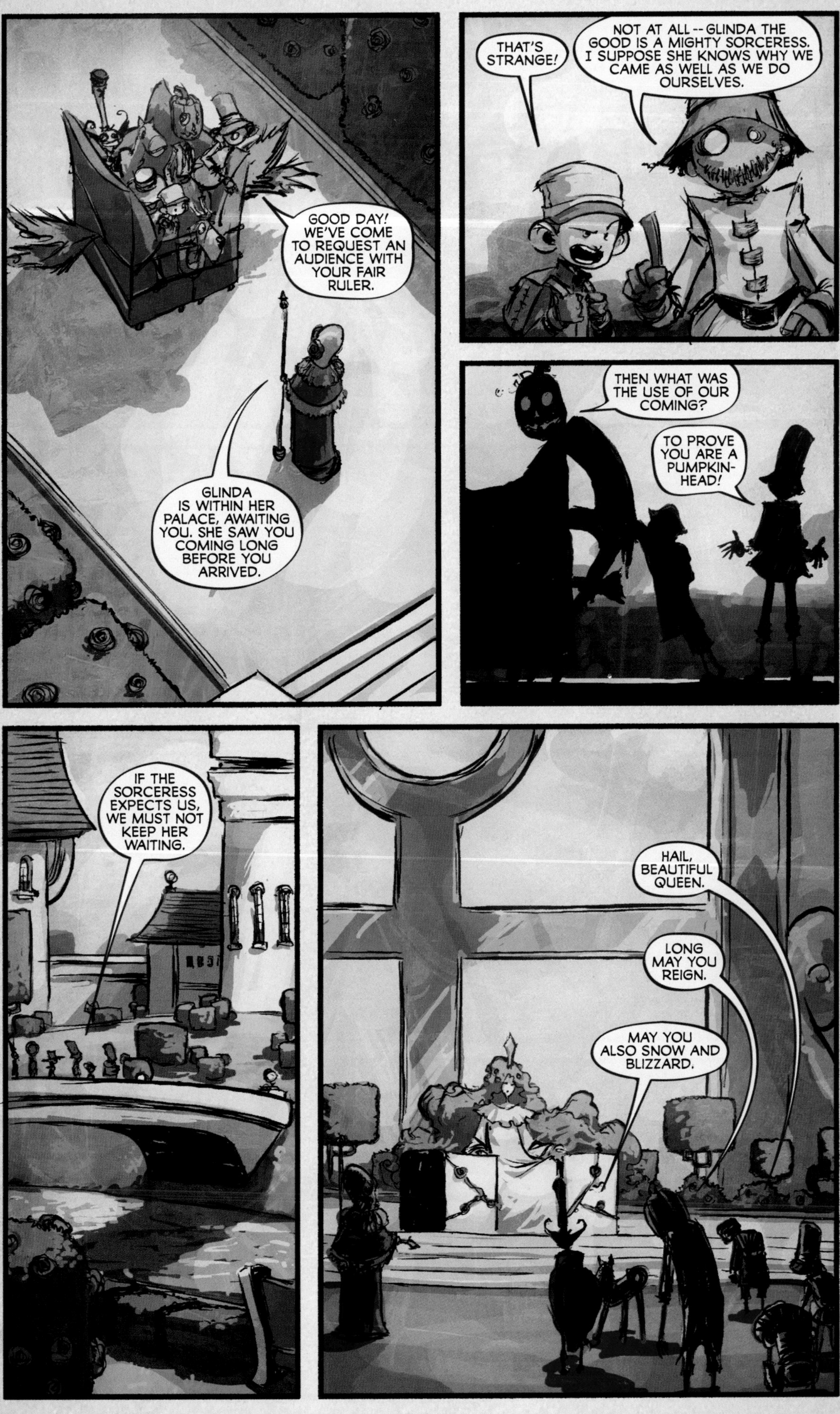

GOOD DAY! WE'VE COME TO REQUEST AN AUDIENCE WITH YOUR FAIR RULER.
GLINDA IS WITHIN HER PALACE, AWAITING YOU. SHE SAW YOU COMING LONG BEFORE YOU ARRIVED.
THAT'S STRANGE!
NOT AT ALL -- GLINDA THE GOOD IS A MIGHTY SORCERESS. I SUPPOSE SHE KNOWS WHY WE CAME AS WELL AS WE DO OURSELVES.
THEN WHAT WAS THE USE OF OUR COMING?
TO PROVE YOU ARE A PUMPKIN-HEAD!
IF THE SORCERESS EXPECTS US, WE MUST NOT KEEP HER WAITING.
HAIL, BEAUTIFUL QUEEN.
LONG MAY YOU REIGN.
MAY YOU ALSO SNOW AND BLIZZARD.

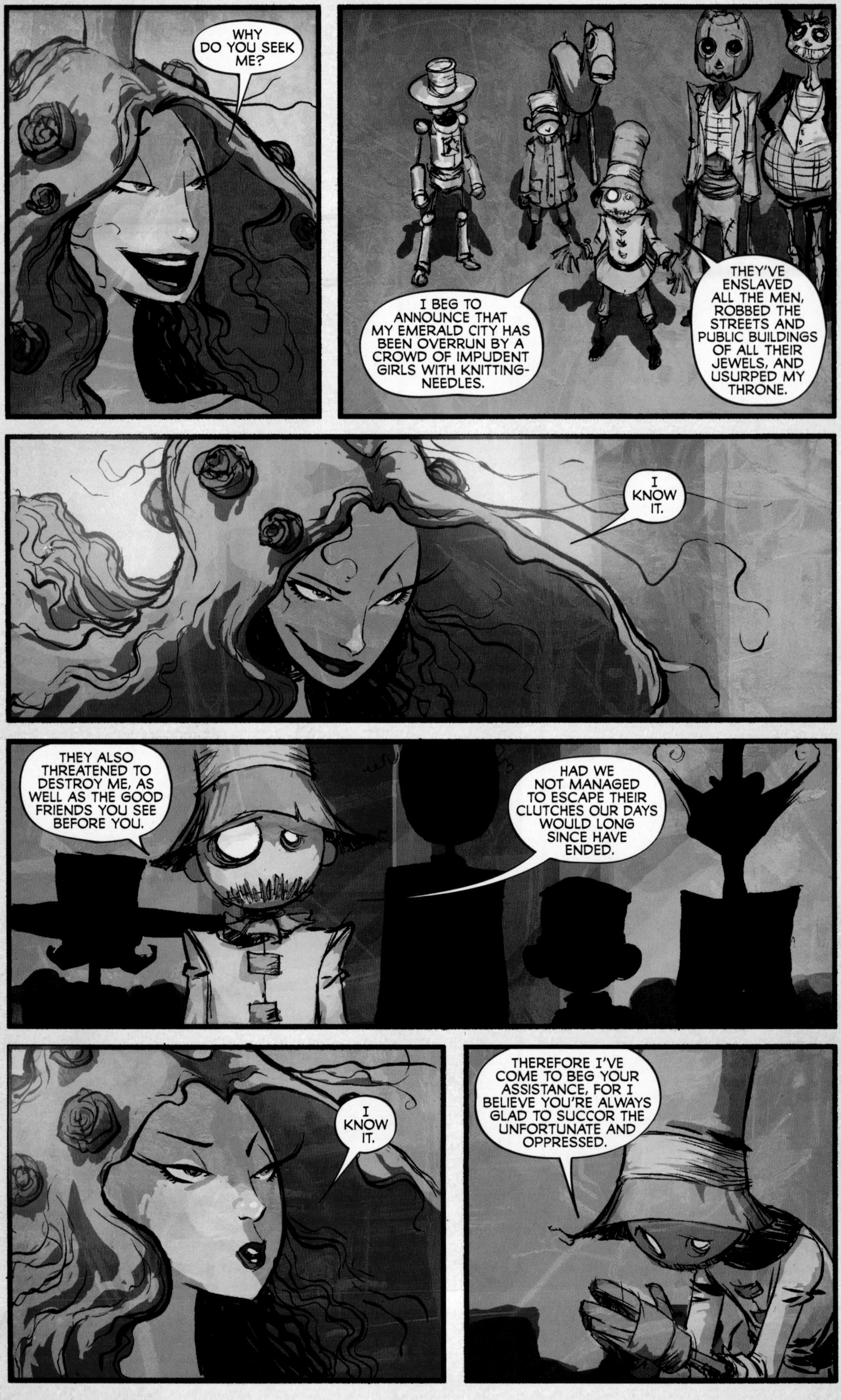
WHY DO YOU SEEK ME?
I BEG TO ANNOUNCE THAT MY EMERALD CITY HAS BEEN OVERRUN BY A CROWD OF IMPUDENT GIRLS WITH KNITTING-NEEDLES.
THEY'VE ENSLAVED ALL THE MEN, ROBBED THE STREETS AND PUBLIC BUILDINGS OF ALL THEIR JEWELS, AND USURPED MY THRONE.
I KNOW IT.
THEY ALSO THREATENED TO DESTROY ME, AS WELL AS THE GOOD FRIENDS YOU SEE BEFORE YOU.
HAD WE NOT MANAGED TO ESCAPE THEIR CLUTCHES OUR DAYS WOULD LONG SINCE HAVE ENDED.
I KNOW IT.
THEREFORE I'VE COME TO BEG YOUR ASSISTANCE, FOR I BELIEVE YOU'RE ALWAYS GLAD TO SUCCOR THE UNFORTUNATE AND OPPRESSED.

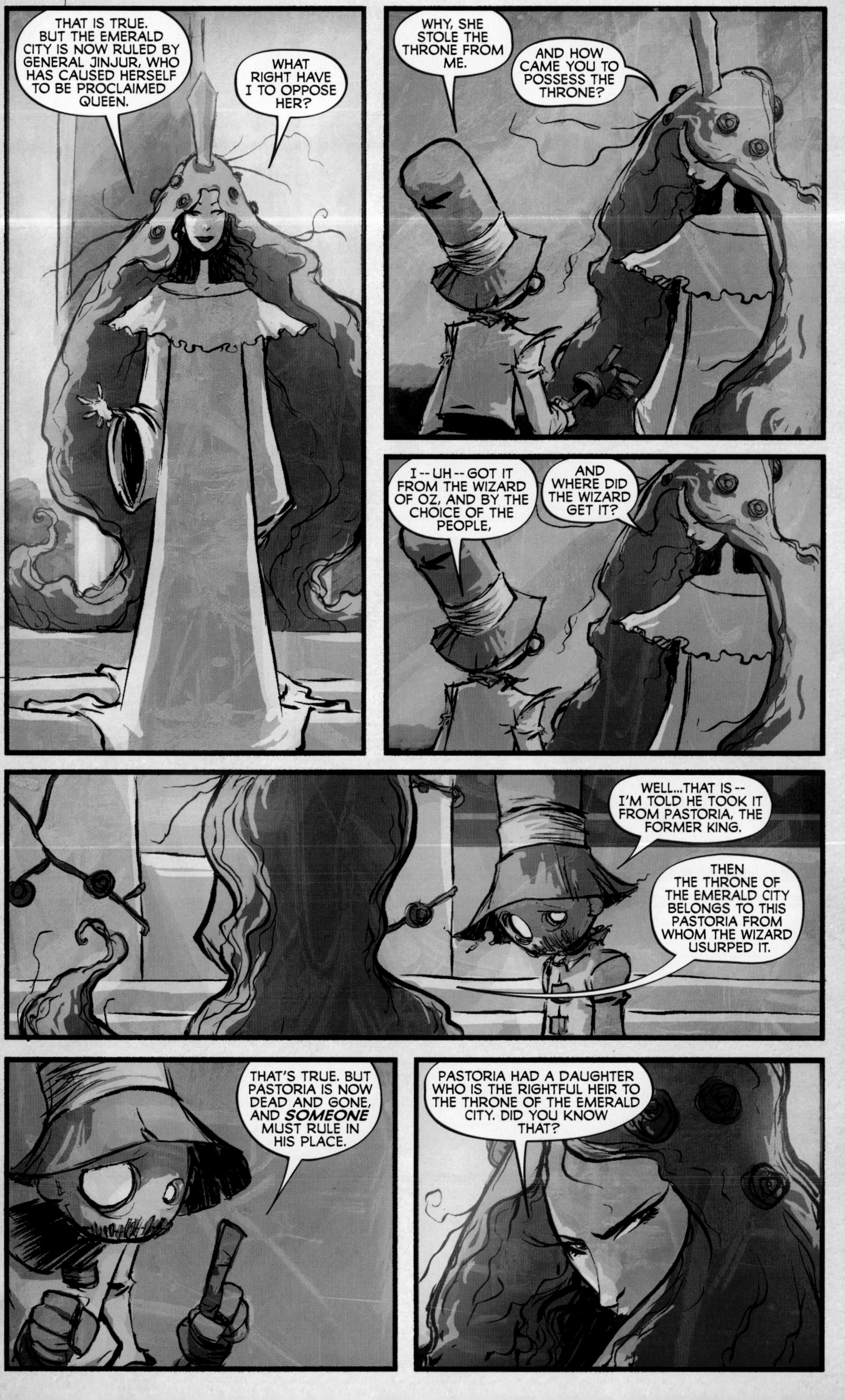
THAT IS TRUE. BUT THE EMERALD CITY IS NOW RULED BY GENERAL JINJUR, WHO HAS CAUSED HERSELF TO BE PROCLAIMED QUEEN.
WHAT RIGHT HAVE I TO OPPOSE HER?
WHY, SHE STOLE THE THRONE FROM ME.
AND HOW CAME YOU TO POSSESS THE THRONE?
I -- UH -- GOT IT FROM THE WIZARD OF OZ, AND BY THE CHOICE OF THE PEOPLE,
AND WHERE DID THE WIZARD GET IT?
WELL...THAT IS -- I'M TOLD HE TOOK IT FROM PASTORIA, THE FORMER KING.
THEN THE THRONE OF THE EMERALD CITY BELONGS TO THIS PASTORIA FROM WHOM THE WIZARD USURPED IT.
THAT'S TRUE. BUT PASTORIA IS NOW DEAD AND GONE, AND ***SOMEONE*** MUST RULE IN HIS PLACE.
PASTORIA HAD A DAUGHTER WHO IS THE RIGHTFUL HEIR TO THE THRONE OF THE EMERALD CITY. DID YOU KNOW THAT?

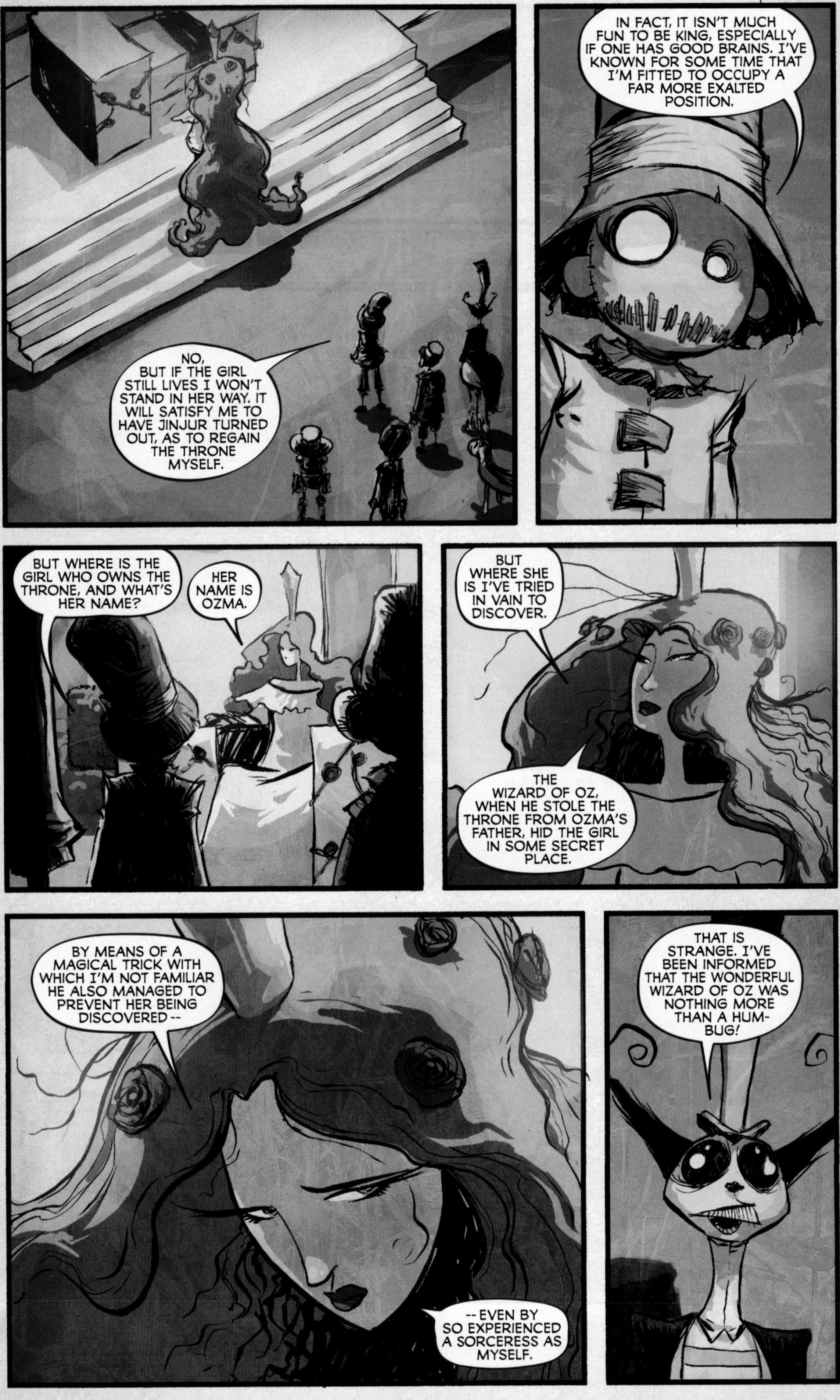
NO, BUT IF THE GIRL STILL LIVES I WON'T STAND IN HER WAY. IT WILL SATISFY ME TO HAVE JINJUR TURNED OUT, AS TO REGAIN THE THRONE MYSELF.
IN FACT, IT ISN'T MUCH FUN TO BE KING, ESPECIALLY IF ONE HAS GOOD BRAINS. I'VE KNOWN FOR SOME TIME THAT I'M FITTED TO OCCUPY A FAR MORE EXALTED POSITION.
BUT WHERE IS THE GIRL WHO OWNS THE THRONE, AND WHAT'S HER NAME?
HER NAME IS OZMA.
BUT WHERE SHE IS I'VE TRIED IN VAIN TO DISCOVER.
THE WIZARD OF OZ, WHEN HE STOLE THE THRONE FROM OZMA'S FATHER, HID THE GIRL IN SOME SECRET PLACE.
BY MEANS OF A MAGICAL TRICK WITH WHICH I'M NOT FAMILIAR HE ALSO MANAGED TO PREVENT HER BEING DISCOVERED--
--EVEN BY SO EXPERIENCED A SORCERESS AS MYSELF.
THAT IS STRANGE. I'VE BEEN INFORMED THAT THE WONDERFUL WIZARD OF OZ WAS NOTHING MORE THAN A HUM-BUG!

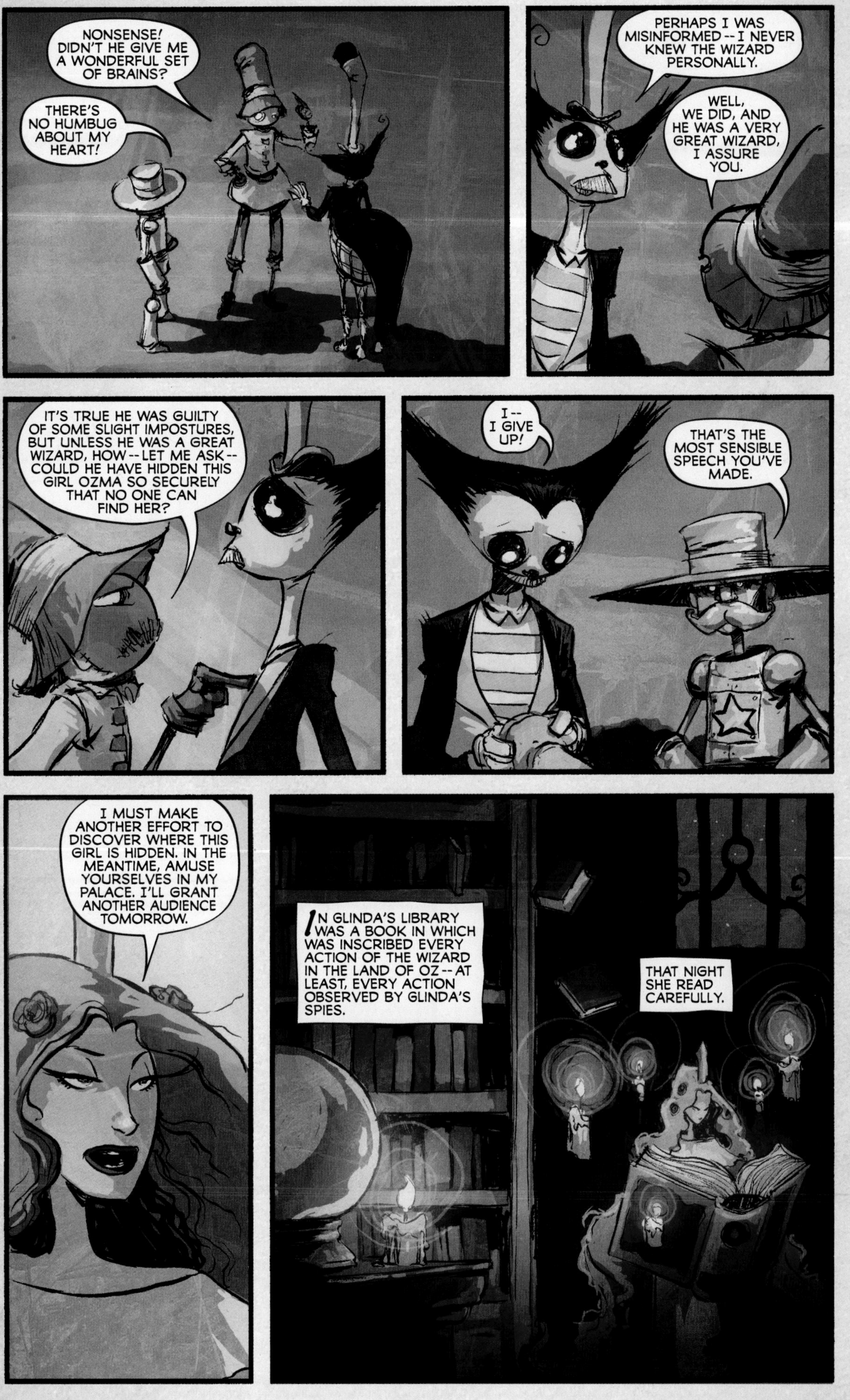
NONSENSE! DIDN'T HE GIVE ME A WONDERFUL SET OF BRAINS?
THERE'S NO HUMBUG ABOUT MY HEART!
PERHAPS I WAS MISINFORMED--I NEVER KNEW THE WIZARD PERSONALLY.
WELL, WE DID, AND HE WAS A VERY GREAT WIZARD, I ASSURE YOU.
IT'S TRUE HE WAS GUILTY OF SOME SLIGHT IMPOSTURES, BUT UNLESS HE WAS A GREAT WIZARD, HOW--LET ME ASK--COULD HE HAVE HIDDEN THIS GIRL OZMA SO SECURELY THAT NO ONE CAN FIND HER?
I-- I GIVE UP!
THAT'S THE MOST SENSIBLE SPEECH YOU'VE MADE.
I MUST MAKE ANOTHER EFFORT TO DISCOVER WHERE THIS GIRL IS HIDDEN. IN THE MEANTIME, AMUSE YOURSELVES IN MY PALACE. I'LL GRANT ANOTHER AUDIENCE TOMORROW.
IN GLINDA'S LIBRARY WAS A BOOK IN WHICH WAS INSCRIBED EVERY ACTION OF THE WIZARD IN THE LAND OF OZ--AT LEAST, EVERY ACTION OBSERVED BY GLINDA'S SPIES.
THAT NIGHT SHE READ CAREFULLY.

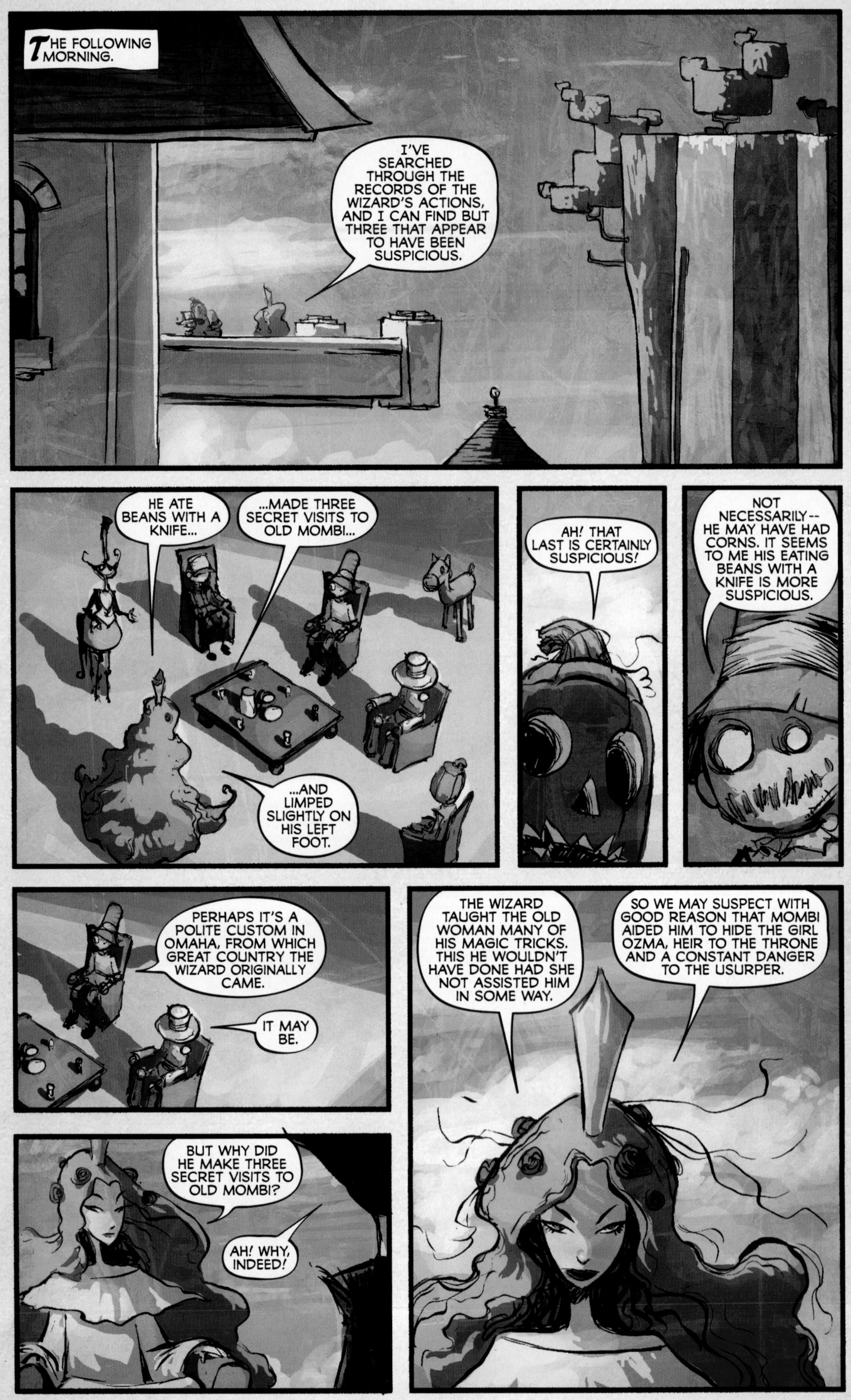
THE FOLLOWING MORNING.
I'VE SEARCHED THROUGH THE RECORDS OF THE WIZARD'S ACTIONS, AND I CAN FIND BUT THREE THAT APPEAR TO HAVE BEEN SUSPICIOUS.
HE ATE BEANS WITH A KNIFE...
...MADE THREE SECRET VISITS TO OLD MOMBI...
...AND LIMPED SLIGHTLY ON HIS LEFT FOOT.
AH! THAT LAST IS CERTAINLY SUSPICIOUS!
NOT NECESSARILY-- HE MAY HAVE HAD CORNS. IT SEEMS TO ME HIS EATING BEANS WITH A KNIFE IS MORE SUSPICIOUS.
PERHAPS IT'S A POLITE CUSTOM IN OMAHA, FROM WHICH GREAT COUNTRY THE WIZARD ORIGINALLY CAME.
IT MAY BE.
BUT WHY DID HE MAKE THREE SECRET VISITS TO OLD MOMBI?
AH! WHY, INDEED!
THE WIZARD TAUGHT THE OLD WOMAN MANY OF HIS MAGIC TRICKS. THIS HE WOULDN'T HAVE DONE HAD SHE NOT ASSISTED HIM IN SOME WAY.
SO WE MAY SUSPECT WITH GOOD REASON THAT MOMBI AIDED HIM TO HIDE THE GIRL OZMA, HEIR TO THE THRONE AND A CONSTANT DANGER TO THE USURPER.

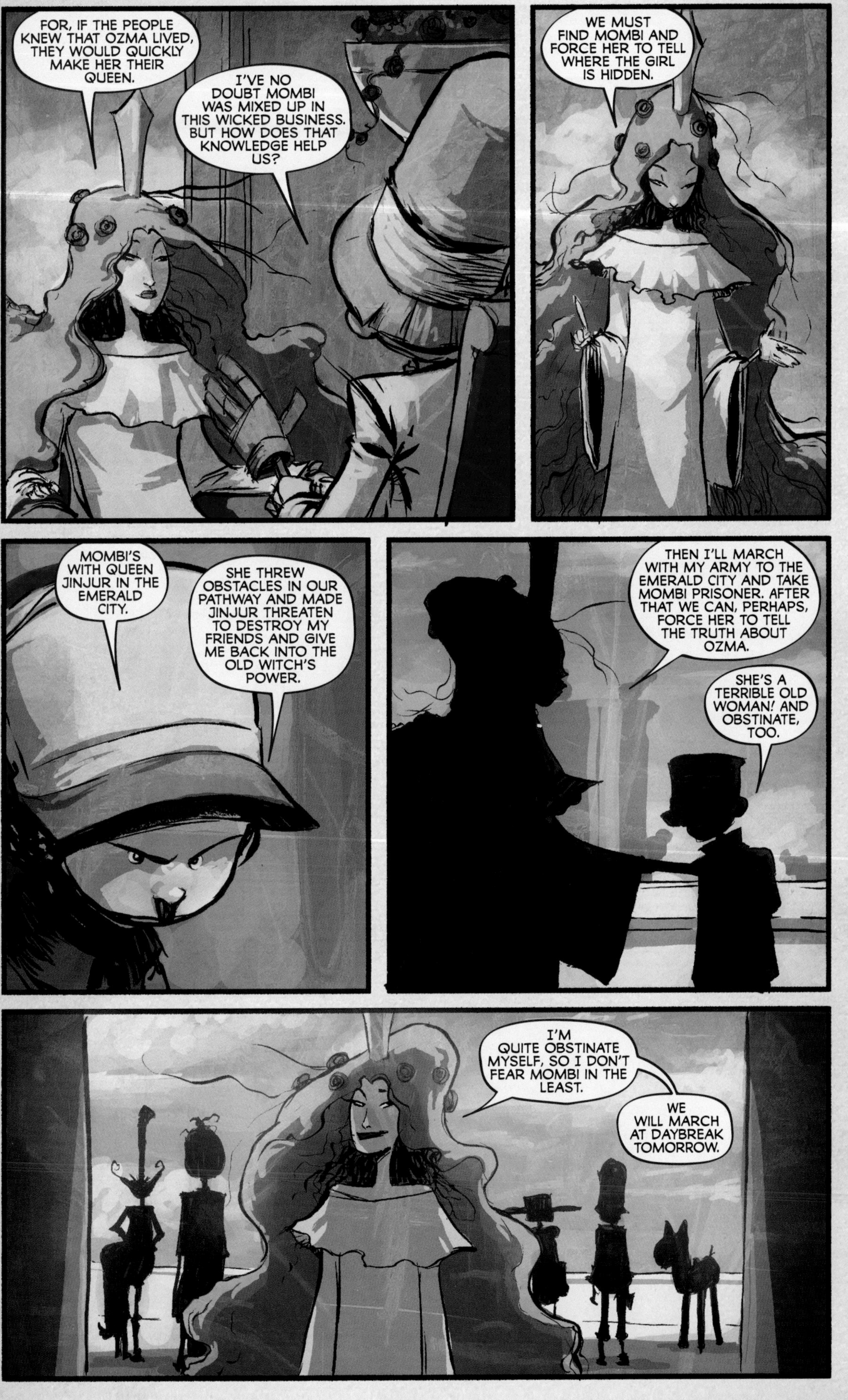

FOR, IF THE PEOPLE KNEW THAT OZMA LIVED, THEY WOULD QUICKLY MAKE HER THEIR QUEEN.
I'VE NO DOUBT MOMBI WAS MIXED UP IN THIS WICKED BUSINESS. BUT HOW DOES THAT KNOWLEDGE HELP US?
WE MUST FIND MOMBI AND FORCE HER TO TELL WHERE THE GIRL IS HIDDEN.
MOMBI'S WITH QUEEN JINJUR IN THE EMERALD CITY.
SHE THREW OBSTACLES IN OUR PATHWAY AND MADE JINJUR THREATEN TO DESTROY MY FRIENDS AND GIVE ME BACK INTO THE OLD WITCH'S POWER.
THEN I'LL MARCH WITH MY ARMY TO THE EMERALD CITY AND TAKE MOMBI PRISONER. AFTER THAT WE CAN, PERHAPS, FORCE HER TO TELL THE TRUTH ABOUT OZMA.
SHE'S A TERRIBLE OLD WOMAN! AND OBSTINATE, TOO.
I'M QUITE OBSTINATE MYSELF, SO I DON'T FEAR MOMBI IN THE LEAST.
WE WILL MARCH AT DAYBREAK TOMORROW.

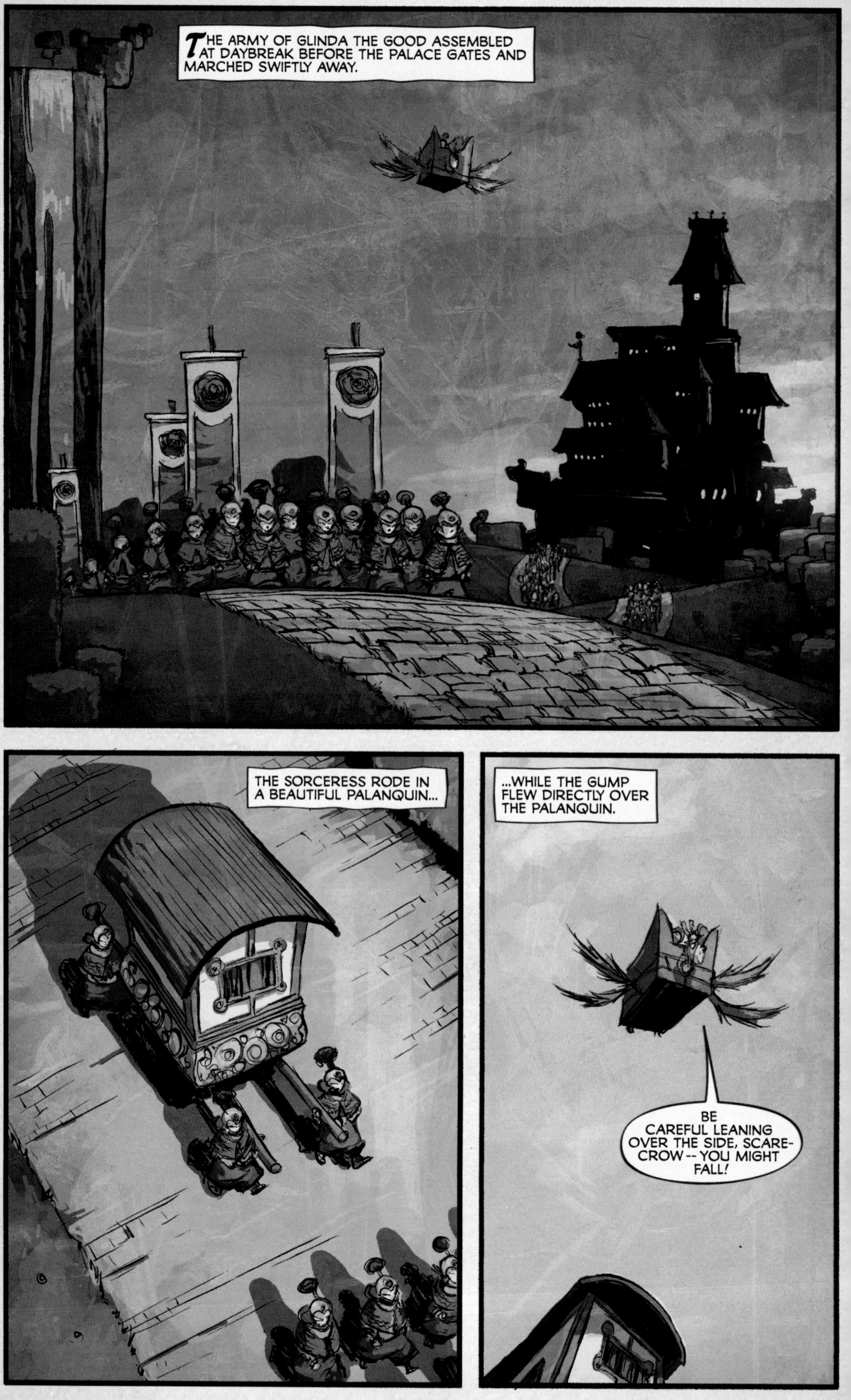
THE ARMY OF GLINDA THE GOOD ASSEMBLED AT DAYBREAK BEFORE THE PALACE GATES AND MARCHED SWIFTLY AWAY.
THE SORCERESS RODE IN A BEAUTIFUL PALANQUIN...
...WHILE THE GUMP FLEW DIRECTLY OVER THE PALANQUIN.
BE CAREFUL LEANING OVER THE SIDE, SCARE-CROW -- YOU MIGHT FALL!

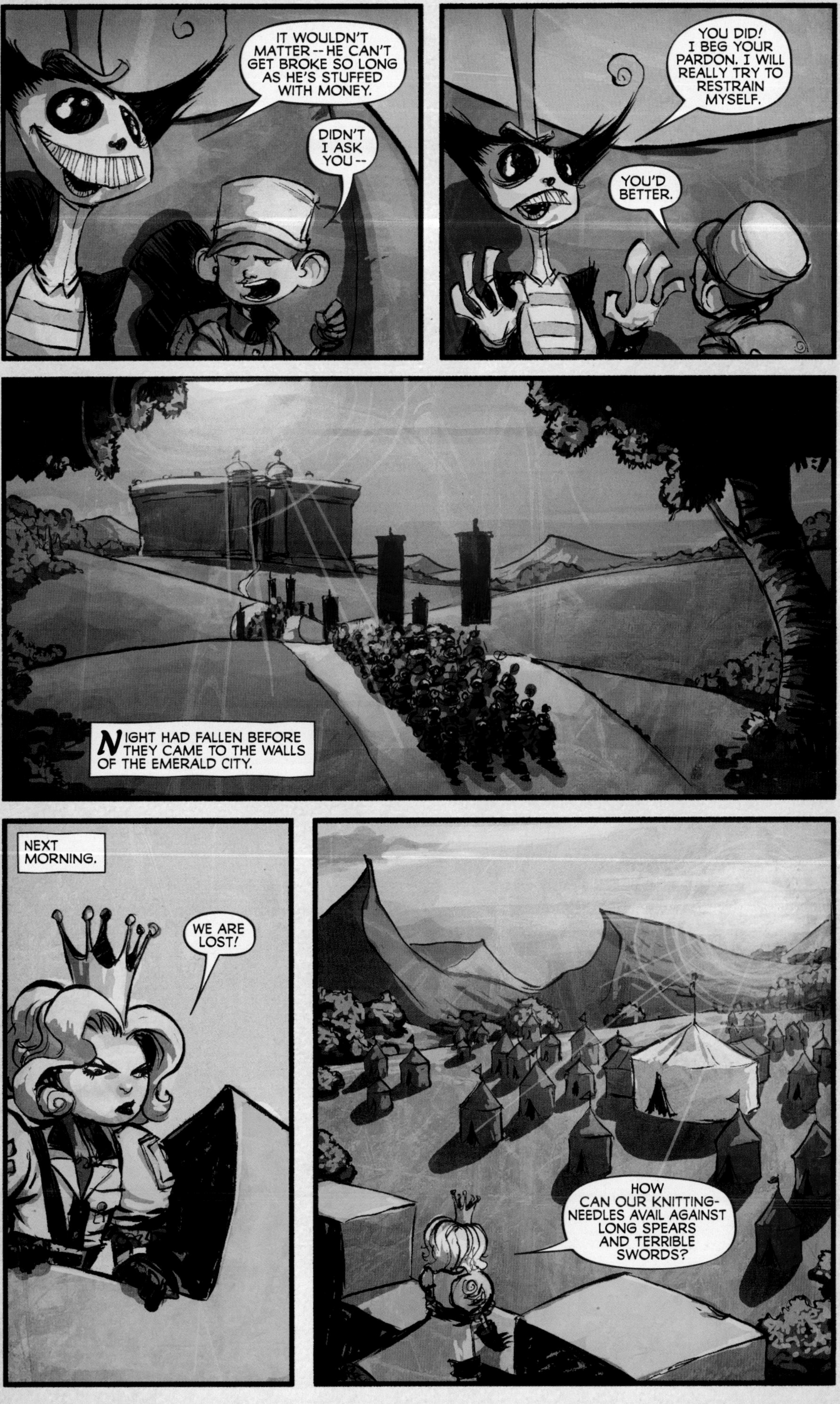
IT WOULDN'T MATTER--HE CAN'T GET BROKE SO LONG AS HE'S STUFFED WITH MONEY.
DIDN'T I ASK YOU--
YOU DID! I BEG YOUR PARDON. I WILL REALLY TRY TO RESTRAIN MYSELF.
YOU'D BETTER.
NIGHT HAD FALLEN BEFORE THEY CAME TO THE WALLS OF THE EMERALD CITY.
NEXT MORNING.
WE ARE LOST!
HOW CAN OUR KNITTING-NEEDLES AVAIL AGAINST LONG SPEARS AND TERRIBLE SWORDS?

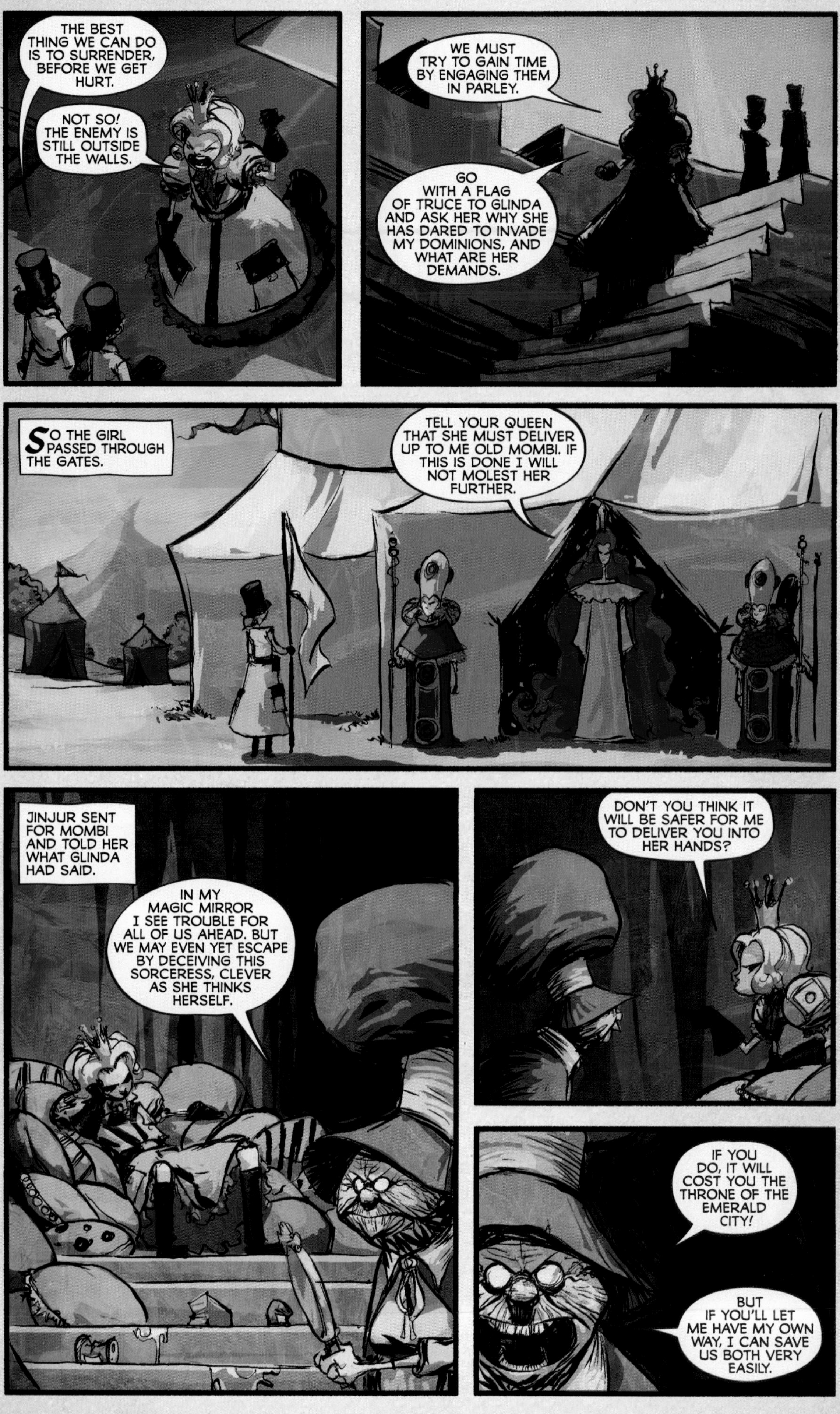
THE BEST THING WE CAN DO IS TO SURRENDER, BEFORE WE GET HURT.
NOT SO! THE ENEMY IS STILL OUTSIDE THE WALLS.
WE MUST TRY TO GAIN TIME BY ENGAGING THEM IN PARLEY.
GO WITH A FLAG OF TRUCE TO GLINDA AND ASK HER WHY SHE HAS DARED TO INVADE MY DOMINIONS, AND WHAT ARE HER DEMANDS.
SO THE GIRL PASSED THROUGH THE GATES.
TELL YOUR QUEEN THAT SHE MUST DELIVER UP TO ME OLD MOMBI. IF THIS IS DONE I WILL NOT MOLEST HER FURTHER.
JINJUR SENT FOR MOMBI AND TOLD HER WHAT GLINDA HAD SAID.
IN MY MAGIC MIRROR I SEE TROUBLE FOR ALL OF US AHEAD. BUT WE MAY EVEN YET ESCAPE BY DECEIVING THIS SORCERESS, CLEVER AS SHE THINKS HERSELF.
DON'T YOU THINK IT WILL BE SAFER FOR ME TO DELIVER YOU INTO HER HANDS?
IF YOU DO, IT WILL COST YOU THE THRONE OF THE EMERALD CITY!
BUT IF YOU'LL LET ME HAVE MY OWN WAY, I CAN SAVE US BOTH VERY EASILY.

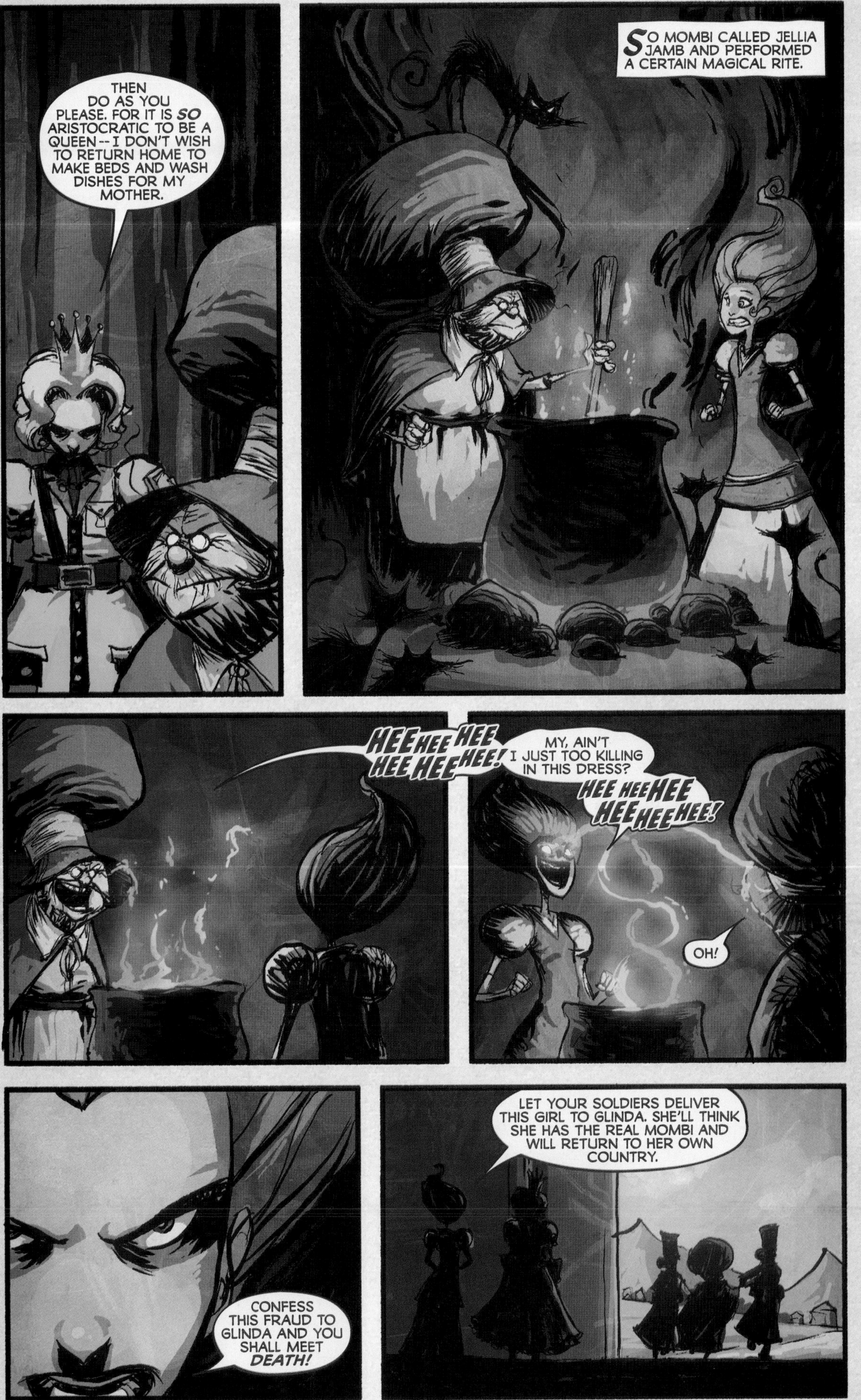
THEN DO AS YOU PLEASE. FOR IT IS *SO* ARISTOCRATIC TO BE A QUEEN-- I DON'T WISH TO RETURN HOME TO MAKE BEDS AND WASH DISHES FOR MY MOTHER.
SO MOMBI CALLED JELLIA JAMB AND PERFORMED A CERTAIN MAGICAL RITE.
HEE HEE HEE HEE HEE HEE!
MY, AIN'T I JUST TOO KILLING IN THIS DRESS?
HEE HEE HEE HEE HEE HEE!
OH!
CONFESS THIS FRAUD TO GLINDA AND YOU SHALL MEET *DEATH!*
LET YOUR SOLDIERS DELIVER THIS GIRL TO GLINDA. SHE'LL THINK SHE HAS THE REAL MOMBI AND WILL RETURN TO HER OWN COUNTRY.

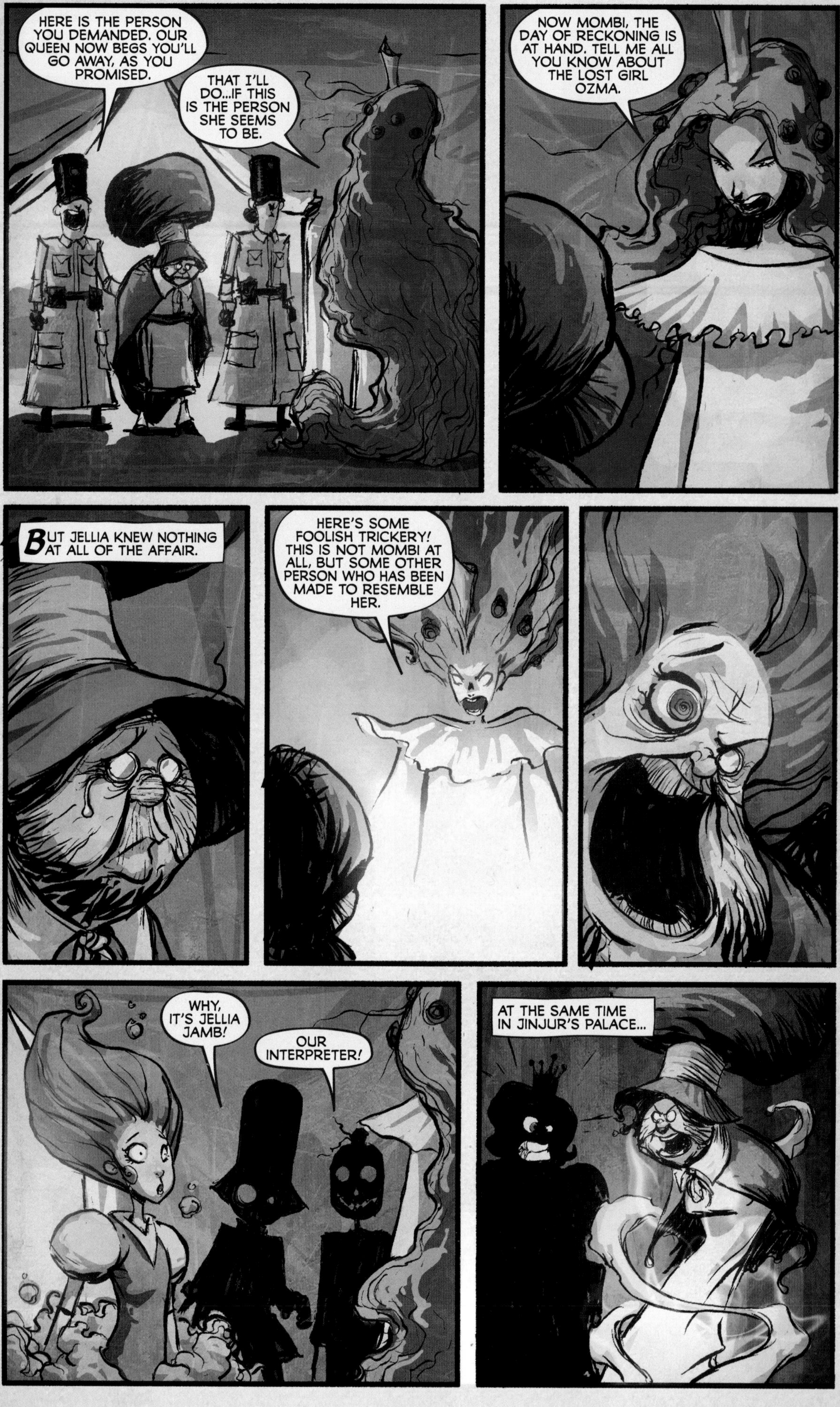
HERE IS THE PERSON YOU DEMANDED. OUR QUEEN NOW BEGS YOU'LL GO AWAY, AS YOU PROMISED.
THAT I'LL DO...IF THIS IS THE PERSON SHE SEEMS TO BE.
NOW MOMBI, THE DAY OF RECKONING IS AT HAND. TELL ME ALL YOU KNOW ABOUT THE LOST GIRL OZMA.
BUT JELLIA KNEW NOTHING AT ALL OF THE AFFAIR.
HERE'S SOME FOOLISH TRICKERY! THIS IS NOT MOMBI AT ALL, BUT SOME OTHER PERSON WHO HAS BEEN MADE TO RESEMBLE HER.
WHY, IT'S JELLIA JAMB!
OUR INTERPRETER!
AT THE SAME TIME IN JINJUR'S PALACE...

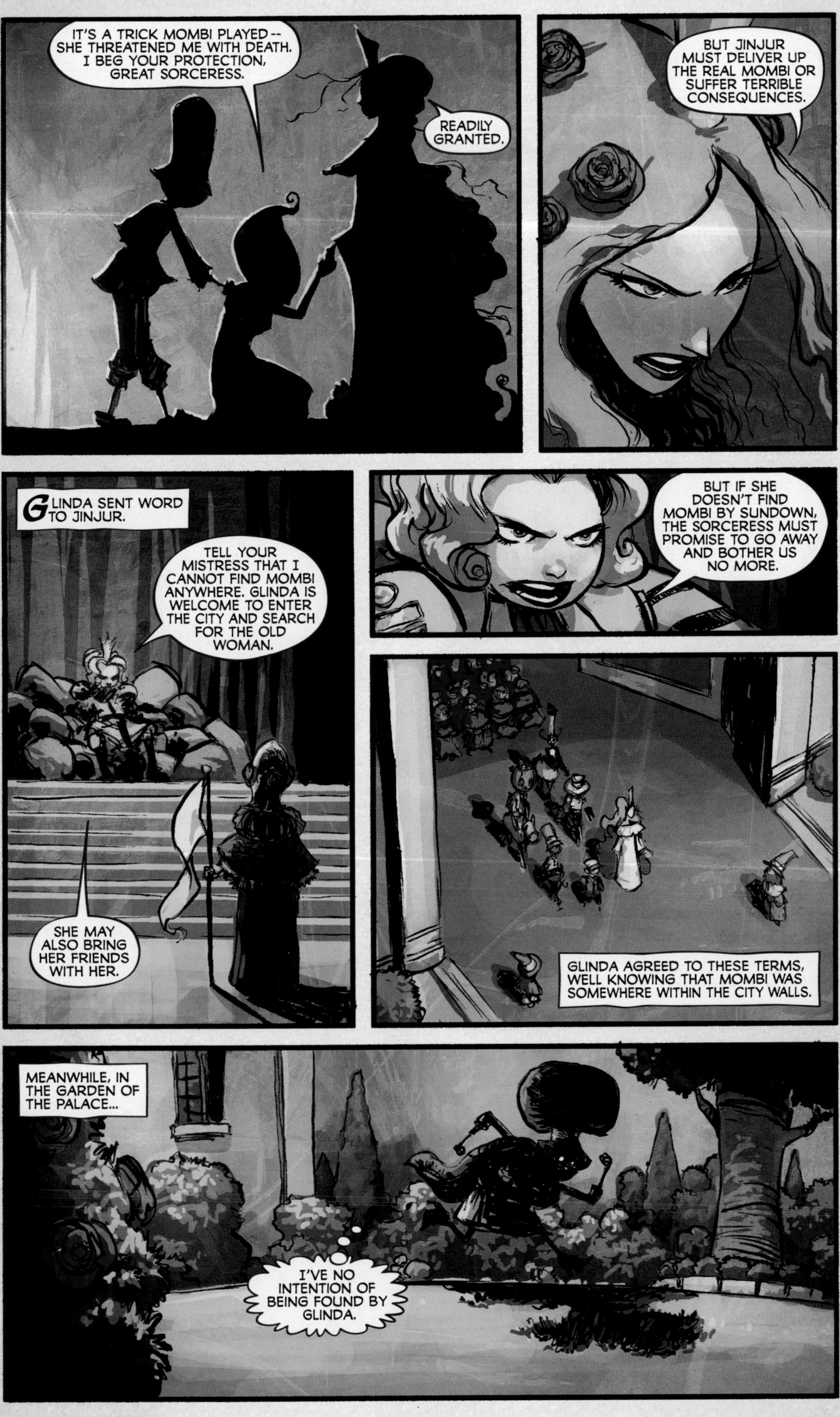
IT'S A TRICK MOMBI PLAYED-- SHE THREATENED ME WITH DEATH. I BEG YOUR PROTECTION, GREAT SORCERESS.
READILY GRANTED.
BUT JINJUR MUST DELIVER UP THE REAL MOMBI OR SUFFER TERRIBLE CONSEQUENCES.
GLINDA SENT WORD TO JINJUR.
TELL YOUR MISTRESS THAT I CANNOT FIND MOMBI ANYWHERE. GLINDA IS WELCOME TO ENTER THE CITY AND SEARCH FOR THE OLD WOMAN.
SHE MAY ALSO BRING HER FRIENDS WITH HER.
BUT IF SHE DOESN'T FIND MOMBI BY SUNDOWN, THE SORCERESS MUST PROMISE TO GO AWAY AND BOTHER US NO MORE.
GLINDA AGREED TO THESE TERMS, WELL KNOWING THAT MOMBI WAS SOMEWHERE WITHIN THE CITY WALLS.
MEANWHILE, IN THE GARDEN OF THE PALACE...
I'VE NO INTENTION OF BEING FOUND BY GLINDA.

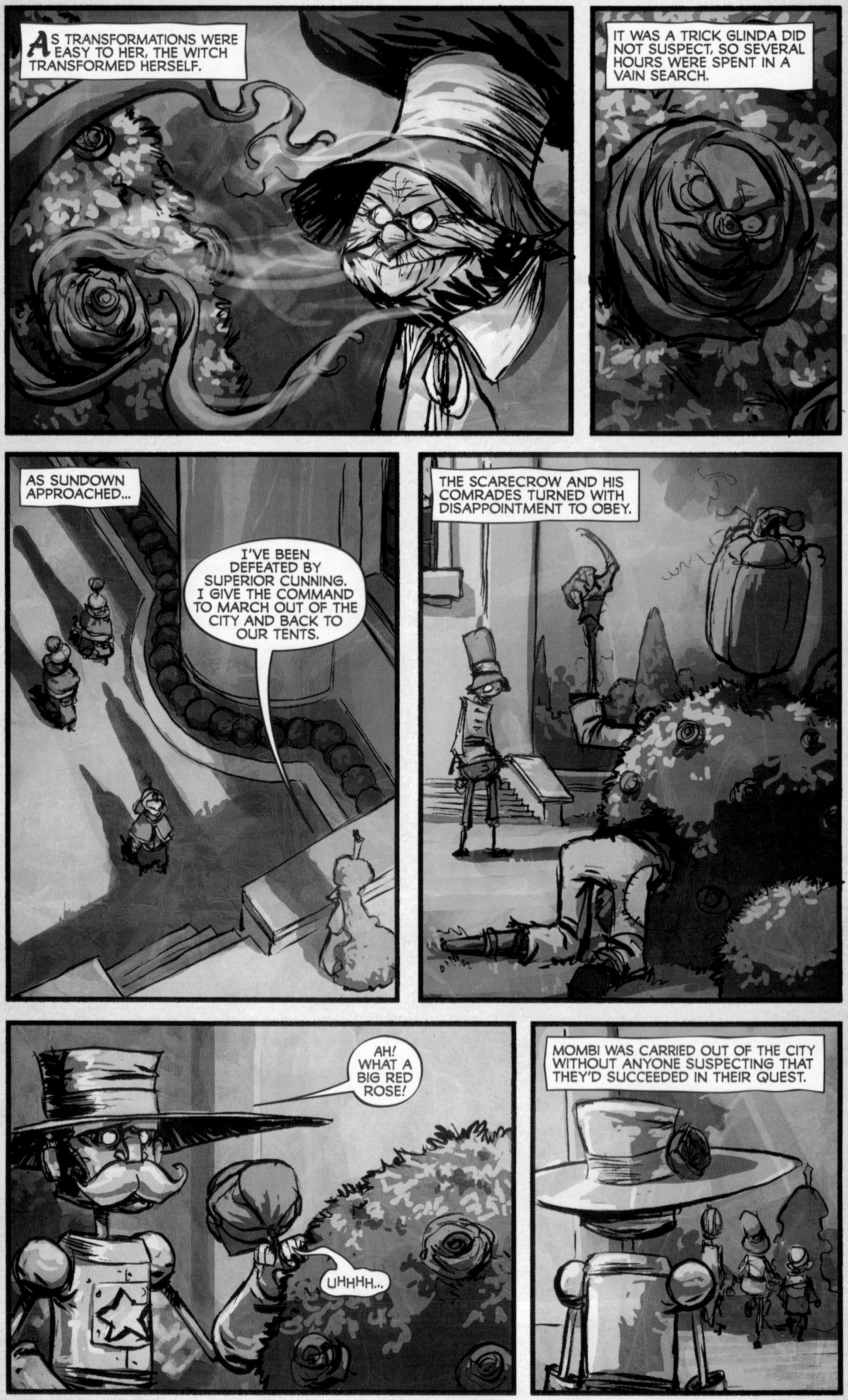
AS TRANSFORMATIONS WERE EASY TO HER, THE WITCH TRANSFORMED HERSELF.
IT WAS A TRICK GLINDA DID NOT SUSPECT, SO SEVERAL HOURS WERE SPENT IN A VAIN SEARCH.
AS SUNDOWN APPROACHED...
I'VE BEEN DEFEATED BY SUPERIOR CUNNING. I GIVE THE COMMAND TO MARCH OUT OF THE CITY AND BACK TO OUR TENTS.
THE SCARECROW AND HIS COMRADES TURNED WITH DISAPPOINTMENT TO OBEY.
AH! WHAT A BIG RED ROSE!
UHHHH...
MOMBI WAS CARRIED OUT OF THE CITY WITHOUT ANYONE SUSPECTING THAT THEY'D SUCCEEDED IN THEIR QUEST.